Figaro

Excitable and ready for adventure, Figaro knows
the neighbourhood like the back of his paw.

Pixie

Pixie has a nose for trouble
and a very active imagination!

Katsumi

Sleek and sophisticated,
Katsumi is quick to call Kitty
at the first sign of trouble.

For Nikki Bloomer, a brilliant bookseller
and all-round amazing lady - P.H.

For Marvin, spreader of joy and
lover of cucumber - J.L.

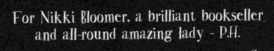

OXFORD
UNIVERSITY PRESS

Great Clarendon Street, Oxford OX2 6DP

Oxford University Press is a department of the University of Oxford.
It furthers the University's objective of excellence in research, scholarship, and
education by publishing worldwide. Oxford is a registered trade mark of Oxford
University Press in the UK and in certain other countries

Text copyright © Paula Harrison 2021
Illustrations copyright © Jenny Løvlie 2021

The moral rights of the author/illustrator have been asserted
Database right Oxford University Press (maker)

First published 2021

British Library Cataloguing in Publication Data

Data available

ISBN: 978-0-19-277784-3

1 3 5 7 9 10 8 6 4 2

Printed in China

Paper used in the production of this book is a natural,
recyclable product made from wood grown in sustainable
forests.The manufacturing process conforms to
the environmentalregulations of the
country of origin.

Kitty

and the
Kidnap Trap

OXFORD
UNIVERSITY PRESS

Chapter

1

'Have you brought your new
hamster home yet?' Kitty asked her
friend, Emily.

They were sitting in the dining hall
at school, having lunch together. Emily
took a spoonful of strawberry yoghurt,

her eyes bright with excitement. 'We fetched him from the animal shelter yesterday. He has the softest white fur you can imagine and when he curls up to go to sleep he looks like a little ball of fluff! He sleeps a lot actually.'

Kitty smiled. She knew how wonderful it was to have a special animal to look after. Pumpkin, her stripy ginger kitten, was more like her best friend than her pet. She had rescued him from a clock tower when he was little and he had lived with her family ever since.

'I'm calling him Marvin,' Emily added.

Kitty finished her apple juice and closed her lunchbox. 'I'd love to meet him. He sounds adorable!'

'I'll ask my mum if you can come

round,' Emily said eagerly. Then her face fell. 'But it can't be this weekend because we're going to visit my gran and we won't be back till Sunday night. I'm a bit worried about leaving Marvin actually. My parents have said I can leave him with plenty of food so he won't go hungry, but what if he gets lonely? And what if he runs out of cucumber? It's his favourite food.'

'Why don't I

visit him while you're away?' said Kitty.
'Then I can give him extra cucumber.'

'That would be great!' said Emily,
cheering up.

'I'll have to ask my mum and dad,
but I'm sure they won't mind. They
love animals.' Kitty smiled as they
headed for the playground. There was
a special reason that her family liked
animals so much.

Kitty, her mum, and her little
brother all had cat-like superpowers.
Kitty could run and jump and balance

just like a cat. She also had super powered hearing and brilliant night vision. Best of all, she could talk to animals and understand what they said. She was still training to be a superhero, but she was always looking for a chance to help others even if it was just offering extra cucumber!

'Emily's house is the one with the pink rose bush,' said Kitty, leading her dad and her little brother, Max, down the street the next day.

Her mum and dad had agreed that she could help out with the hamster and Emily's parents had dropped off the house keys that morning. Kitty opened the gate and ran up the path to Emily's front door.

'We'll stay downstairs,' Dad told Kitty, as he unlocked the door. 'Take your time and check that the hamster has everything he needs.'

'Thanks, Dad!' Kitty ran to the fridge and took out a box of cucumber sticks. Then she ran lightly up the stairs.

Kitty had been to Emily's house lots of times but she'd never met Marvin before. The little hamster was running inside his wheel, his tiny feet pattering up and down.

Kitty crouched beside his cage and smiled. 'Hello, Marvin. My name's Kitty and I've come to look after you while Emily's away.'

Marvin didn't
stop to look at
Kitty. The wheel
squeaked as he ran.

'I'm going to change your food and
water,' Kitty added. 'Then maybe you'd
like some cucumber?' She opened the
little hatch to the cage and changed
the food. Then she took out the water
bottle and refilled that too. Finally,
she opened the box of cucumber and
placed a few sticks inside the cage.

'Will that be enough?' she asked

Marvin. 'Emily didn't say how much you eat.'

Marvin didn't turn round or prick up his ears. He just went on running. Kitty frowned. It seemed odd that Marvin was exercising so much when Emily had talked about how sleepy he was. Maybe he was worried about being left by himself?

She crouched down by the cage again. 'Listen, everything will be all right!' she said gently. 'Emily will be back really soon.'

Marvin's feet pattered on the little
wheel.

'She's only away till tomorrow
evening,' Kitty tried again. 'I know she
loves looking after you.'

Marvin made no reply. His whiskers quivered as he ran. He had a glazed look as he stared through the window straight ahead.

Kitty watched him, uncertainly. She felt sure something was wrong. 'Are you OK? If there's something else you need I can fetch it for you.'

She was wondering what else to say when Dad called up the stairs. 'Is everything all right, Kitty?'

'I'm coming.' Kitty rubbed her cheek worriedly. Then she picked up the cucumber box. She couldn't force Marvin to talk if he didn't want to. 'Bye Marvin, I hope you enjoy your cucumber.' She took one last look at the hamster before heading downstairs.

'I'm hungry! Can we have pizza for lunch?' Max asked Dad as they left.

'Maybe,' said Dad. 'Would you like that too, Kitty?'

Kitty nodded but she wasn't really listening properly. She was thinking about Marvin. With her super hearing, she could still hear the hamster's wheel

spinning as they walked

away down the street.

Chapter 2

Kitty climbed into bed and snuggled down under her blanket that night. A huge full moon was shining in at the window and casting a beam of silvery light across the floor. Pumpkin settled down on the pillow beside her

with his stripy head pressed against her cheek.

'Night, Pumpkin.' Kitty closed her eyes and waited for sleep to come.

The wind rustled the tree outside the window. A branch squeaked against the glass and Kitty's eyes flew open again. That squeaky sound made her think of Marvin's wheel. She couldn't help feeling worried about the little hamster.

'What's wrong, Kitty?' mewed Pumpkin. 'Why do you keep wriggling?'

'I'm thinking about Emily's hamster,' said Kitty. 'He wouldn't speak to me this morning.

He just kept running the whole time.'

'Hamsters are very strange animals! You wouldn't catch me racing around a wheel all day.' Pumpkin snuggled down against the pillow.

Kitty lay still for a moment, thinking. Then she sat up in bed. 'I'd better go and check he's all right. After all, Emily trusted me to look after him.' She leapt out of bed and grabbed her superhero outfit. Then she put on her cat ears and mask, before tying her cape around her neck.

'But it's so warm and cozy in here! I don't want to go out in the dark,' Pumpkin protested, burrowing under the blanket.

'It's all right, Pumpkin, I won't be long,' said Kitty. 'I'll just run along the rooftop and look in at Emily's window. If Marvin's asleep safe and sound, I'll come straight back again.'

Pumpkin reluctantly climbed out from under the blanket. 'But then you'll have an exciting time without me! I guess I'll come. I hope it's not too far though.'

Kitty pulled back her curtain. A warm breath of air swirled in as she opened the window. A fox barked somewhere in the distance

and there was the faint rumble of
a motorbike. The full moon hung
low and the stars glittered across
the night sky. Kitty's skin prickled
with excitement. She felt as though
adventure was calling to her!

She scrambled out of the window, followed by Pumpkin. Together they climbed to the rooftop and gazed all around. Kitty loved being high above the street, especially when everything looked so silvery and beautiful in the moonlight. She tried to remember the way to Emily's house. She had never been there using the rooftops before.

Then her super senses began to work and she recognized the scent of the rose bush by Emily's front door. She could see the end of her friend's street with her special night vision.

Her superpowers tingled inside her as she ran along the rooftop. Then she leapt from one roof to the next with her cloak flying out around her. She turned back to catch Pumpkin as he jumped over the gap.

Emily's house was only three streets along. Kitty skipped around the chimney pot and clambered down to the edge of the roof. Peering into the garden, she checked for the rose bush. Yes, this was Emily's house!

Kitty climbed down the drainpipe,

whispering, 'wait for me here, Pumpkin!'

She swung across to the windowsill and pulled herself up. Then she cupped her hand to the window and peeped through the glass. A shadow lay over Marvin's cage and there was no sign of the little hamster. Maybe he'd stopped running and gone to sleep at last!

Kitty peered at the cage. Was
Marvin curled up under his bedding
somewhere? There were lumps in the
sawdust but none of them had a furry
white nose or a tiny foot sticking out.

Then Kitty noticed the cage door was ajar. Her stomach lurched horribly. Marvin had gone!

She climbed quickly back onto the roof. 'Marvin isn't inside his cage anymore,' she told Pumpkin. 'I have to find him!'

Kitty headed for an open skylight. Lowering herself through the window, she dropped on to the bathroom floor and reached for Pumpkin. Together they dashed down the hall to Emily's bedroom. Kitty crouched beside the open cage door. She knew she had fastened it tightly that morning. Had Marvin worked out how to open it or had someone broken in and taken him?

'Marvin, are you here?' she called softly. 'It's me, Kitty. I brought you the cucumber this morning.'

There was no answer. Kitty used her super hearing to listen very carefully, but she couldn't hear any rustling or tiny feet pattering across the carpet. All she could hear was a clock ticking downstairs and the fridge whirring in the kitchen.

'Maybe he's hiding somewhere,' Pumpkin suggested. 'Hamsters are small enough to fit into all kinds of hidey-holes.'

'You're right! We'd better check the whole house.' Kitty dashed to the next bedroom while Pumpkin scampered downstairs.

Kitty checked every corner of the upstairs. There was still no sign of Marvin.

'Look at this, Kitty!' called Pumpkin.

Kitty found Pumpkin in the living room standing beside the fruit bowl. There were tiny teeth marks in one of the apples and some of the grapes had been knocked out of the bowl as if the hamster had run away in a hurry.

Kitty noticed a sticky-sweet trail across the carpet. Marvin must have got some of the apple on his feet. Using her cat-like eyesight and sense of smell, Kitty followed the sticky footprints down the hallway to the kitchen. Some cups had been knocked over on the worktop.

'Why did Marvin make such a mess?' wondered Pumpkin.

'I don't know.' Kitty followed the footprints across the room. They led to the back door and vanished by a small crack in the door frame.

Kitty caught her breath.
It was a tiny hole but it was
certainly big enough for a
hamster.

Marvin had escaped
from the house and run
away into the darkness.

Chapter 3

Kitty stared at the crack in the door frame. 'Oh no! Emily will be so upset when she finds out Marvin is gone.'

'But why would he run away?' asked Pumpkin. 'Wasn't Emily looking after him properly?'

'Of course she was!' said Kitty.

'Then maybe he's a reckless sort of animal who does what he likes and never thinks of anyone else.' Pumpkin twitched his whiskers disapprovingly. '*I* would never be like that!'

Kitty thought of Marvin running wildly in his wheel that morning. There was certainly something strange about his behaviour. 'I think we have to find him and ask him why he ran away. I just hope he talks to me this time.'

Pumpkin and Kitty ran back

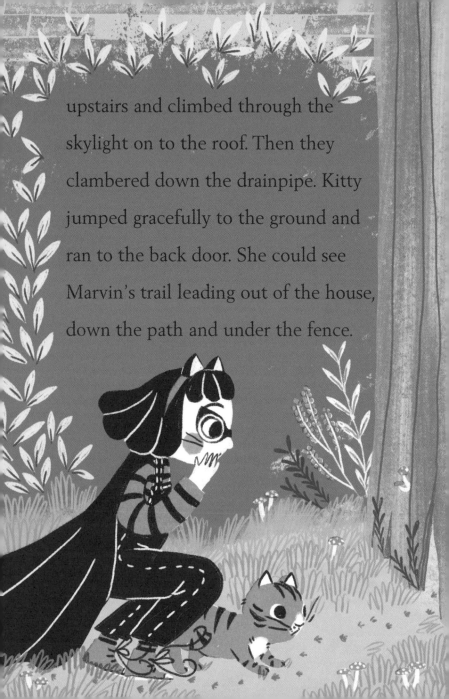

upstairs and climbed through the
skylight on to the roof. Then they
clambered down the drainpipe. Kitty
jumped gracefully to the ground and
ran to the back door. She could see
Marvin's trail leading out of the house,
down the path and under the fence.

'This way, Pumpkin!' She clambered over the fence, lifting the ginger kitten after her.

Marvin's trail led along the street and down the alley. Then the sticky footprints began weaving around in little circles as if Marvin hadn't been sure which way he wanted to go. At last the prints grew fainter and disappeared under a bush. Kitty searched through the leaves but there was no sign of Marvin anywhere.

'Now what do we do?' Pumpkin flopped onto the pavement. 'If only the hamster had stayed at home! We could have been back in our cozy beds by now.'

Kitty pointed to the end of the street. A church with a tall spire stood on the corner. 'Let's try this way. Maybe we'll be able to pick up the trail again.' She raced up the road with Pumpkin close behind her.

They ran into Kitty's friend, Figaro, right outside the church gate. His black-and-white coat was ruffled. 'Good evening, Kitty!' he mewed. 'I see I'm not the only one who can't sleep.'

'Hello, Figaro!' Kitty said, breathlessly. 'Did you see a little white hamster pass this way?'

'No, I'm afraid not!' Figaro replied. 'I saw a gang of rowdy rats though. They were swaggering up and down the street for ages. I can't believe such tiny creatures could make such a ruckus! They woke me from a lovely dream about eating fried cod in a herb sauce. I'm looking for them right now so I can tell them *exactly* what I think of them!' He twitched his whiskers crossly.

'I wonder if they've seen Marvin.' Kitty quickly explained to Figaro about the hamster's escape. 'Let's track them down together. Which way did they go?'

Figaro rubbed his eyes. 'I have no idea. I'm so tired I can hardly hold my whiskers up! I need a nice long sleep.'

'Me too,' said Pumpkin wistfully.

Kitty listened carefully using her super hearing. The rats might be able to help her, but she would have to find them quickly. She could hear creatures squeaking in the distance but which way had they gone? It was hard to be sure with the wind rustling the trees so much.

'I'll see if I can spot them from the church spire,' she told the others. 'Wait for me here.'

Hurrying over to a
drainpipe, she climbed onto
the church roof and began
clambering up the tower.

The wind blew strongly, making her cape fly out around her. Rough tiles lined the spire, giving her plenty of handholds and footholds as she pulled herself to the top.

Clutching the spire with one arm, Kitty gazed at Hallam City far below. Streets and alleyways crisscrossed the whole city and rows of houses stretched as far as she could see. The rats were scampering along an alley close to the river. Kitty's heart lifted. If they had been wandering around all night, they were sure to have seen Marvin.

Sliding down the spire, she ran
across the church roof and then
made her way to the ground
where Pumpkin and Figaro
were waiting. 'I've found
the rats!' she cried. 'We
need to get their help
right away.'

'I'm not sure they're the helpful sort,' Figaro began, grumpily.

Kitty didn't wait to hear what else he was saying. She hurried down the street and raced along the alleyway. The alley led into Waterbury Avenue and Kitty spotted the rats not far away. They were heading for the cafes that lined the riverside, with neat rows of

tables set out on the pavement.
The river gleamed at the bottom of
the grassy bank, lit up by the moon
like a sheet of silver paper.

The rats stopped beside the
Cookies and Cream Café and one
of the creatures scrambled on to
an outdoor table. She was

bigger than

the others, with large ears and a crooked tail. Pointing at the *Closed* sign on the café door,

she squeaked excitedly. Kitty slipped closer, trying to hear, but the rat's words were lost under the gurgling of the river.

Just then she noticed a flash of white fur in the middle of the crowd. The gang of rats moved apart a little and Kitty's gaze fixed on a tiny shape in the middle. She recognized the creature's soft fur and delicate whiskers.

It was Marvin!

Kitty turned to Pumpkin and Figaro, who were still struggling to catch up. 'I've found him!' she said, beaming. 'He was with the rats all the time.'

'Wait, Kitty! Figaro says those rats are very naughty,' called Pumpkin. 'It's all right! I can see Marvin.' Kitty sighed with relief. Marvin was safe after all.

Maybe the little hamster had got lost and the rats were helping him.

She was about to rush over to thank them, when the rat with the crooked tail leapt down from the table. She bounded over to Marvin and began pushing him towards the café door. Marvin squealed in protest and covered his face with his tiny claws.

Kitty watched in shock as the rats gathered round Marvin. Their squeaking grew noisier as if they were all arguing at once. Marvin disappeared among a

mass of rat tails and brown whiskers.

A feeling of dread grew in Kitty's stomach. It didn't seem as if the rats were helping the hamster at all. It looked as if Marvin was in an awful lot of trouble.

Chapter 4

Kitty leapt forwards, her
cape flying. She had to reach Marvin as
fast as she could. The little hamster was
no match for a whole gang of naughty
rats. Running along the riverbank, she
gained speed. The river gurgled beside

her and pale moonlight glittered on
the dark water.

Kitty slowed down when she
reached the row of shops and cafes.

The street was empty. Had the rats heard her coming and run away, taking Marvin with them? Suddenly she noticed the door to the Cookies and Cream Café was ajar.

CRASH! The noise made Kitty jump. It was followed by loud giggling from inside the café.

Kitty crept over to the shop window and peeped in. Rats were running all over the café, playing with the knives and forks, and swinging from the tables. A broken plate lay in pieces on the floor.

The rat leader bounded onto
the counter, waving her crooked tail.
She danced up and down along the
worktop. Then she tore open a sachet
of sugar and poured it into her mouth.
Swallowing it in one gulp, she shouted,
'we're the amazing river rats and we
can do whatever we like. Nothing can
stop us—not even bossy old cats!'

A cheer went up from the other rats and they began singing rowdily.

Kitty crouched low, looking desperately for Marvin. She spotted a tiny ball of fluff huddled under a table. A spoon came crashing down from above and Marvin trembled and clung to the table leg. A pair of rats chased after him and pulled him out.

'Why are you hiding, Marvin?' cried the rat leader. 'You should be joining in with our fun. Try one of these cakes. It's full of sugar!' She waved her

tail at the pink-iced cupcakes behind
the counter.

'You're not supposed to do that,'
squeaked Marvin. 'It's stealing!'

'Oh, don't worry about that!'
The rat grinned widely. 'We go where
we like and we take what we want.
We don't let nothing stop us.'

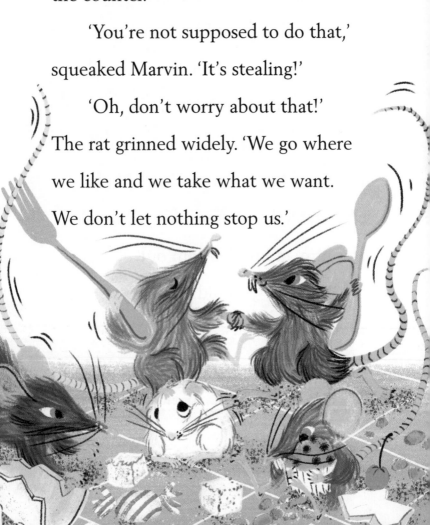

She twirled her wonky tail, knocking over a salt cellar and spilling grains of salt everywhere.

Figaro and Pumpkin caught up with Kitty and peered through the café window.

'You were right about those rats,' Kitty told Figaro. 'Just look at the mess they've made.'

'What on earth do they think they're doing? I'll put a stop to this at once!' Figaro puffed out his chest

63

indignantly as he headed for the café door.

'Wait, Figaro!' Kitty said quickly. 'If they run away Marvin could get trampled in the rush. Let me try talking to them by myself.'

Figaro frowned. 'Very well! But if they don't listen I'm coming inside to pounce on them.'

Another plate crashed to the floor and the rats giggled.

'You'd better hurry!' Pumpkin said, wide-eyed. 'Marvin looks so scared.'

Kitty crept to the café door and opened it slowly. She didn't want to startle the rats. Maybe if she talked to them quietly they would calm down and leave Marvin alone.

Two of the rats had pulled Marvin onto the counter. The rat leader slid open the food cabinet to show him the cupcakes with their gleaming pink icing. Then she pushed him towards a row of chocolate muffins.

'See how yummy everything looks!' she said. 'Don't you want to take a teensy weensy bite?'

'But I don't even like cake!' cried Marvin.

'EVERYONE likes cake!' The rat leader sniffed the nearest muffin, her whiskers quivering. 'Just catch a whiff of that and then take a nice big bite.'

'What I really love is cucumber,' Marvin told her. 'It's juicy and crunchy and . . .'

'CUCUMBER!' yelled the rat leader. 'You can't call yourself a rat if you prefer veggie-yuck to cake.'

'But I'm not a rat! I'm a hamster,' said Marvin. 'I'm sorry but I really think I should be going now . . .'

The rat leader took a huge bite of the chocolate muffin, spilling crumbs all over the counter. The rats began to cheer and Marvin's words were lost beneath the noise.

The leader picked a chocolate chip
out of the muffin and shoved it in her
mouth.

'Ruby Rat! RUBY RAT!' the rats
chanted.

The rat leader grinned and
took a bow. 'Just call me Ruby the
Magnificent, Chief Thief of Hallam
City!'

Marvin crept across the counter and tried to hide behind the till but Ruby hauled him back.

'Listen, lil' friend!' She patted his neck. 'You said you wanted an adventure! You said you wanted to try living like us—going wherever you want and doing whatever you like. Here's your chance! Take a bite of this cake and the rest will be easy!'

Kitty took a step forward. None of the rats had noticed her standing in the shadows by the door. Their eyes were

fixed on Marvin, Ruby, and the muffin.

'I know I wanted an adventure,' quavered Marvin. 'But I don't think I do anymore! I miss my cozy cage and snuggling under the bedding with a nice piece of cucumber . . .'

'What IS cucumber?' a baby rat asked his mother.

'Just a nasty green food,' his mother replied. 'Stick to crisps and sugar and you'll grow big and strong and ratty!'

Ruby towered over Marvin. 'Try it. Just one bite!' Breaking off a chunk of muffin, she pushed it under the hamster's whiskers.

'Stop!' cried Kitty. 'You can't make him eat it if he doesn't want to. Anyway he's right—it's stealing! You shouldn't have broken in here at all.'

71

The rats whipped round in an instant and glared at Kitty.

Ruby pushed Marvin behind her and her dark eyes glinted. 'Careful, guys!' she told the other rats. 'Look at her ears and tail! She's a Cat Girl and that means she's NOT to be trusted.'

Chapter 5

A cluster of rats barred Kitty's way. Some of them scampered onto the counter and formed a ring around Ruby and Marvin.

'Don't come any closer!' one rat said.

'Keep your paws out of our business!' snapped another.

'I just want to talk to you,' Kitty said, over all the noise. 'Marvin, are you all right?'

Marvin shook his head and tried to speak but Ruby stuck her tail over his mouth. 'Cats are nothing but trouble!' she said. 'Don't worry, Marvin. We'll save you from the Bad Cat Girl.'

'I'm not here to hurt anyone!' cried Kitty. 'I'm here because I'm meant to be taking care of Marvin while my friend's away.'

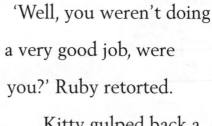

'Well, you weren't doing a very good job, were you?' Ruby retorted.

Kitty gulped back a

reply. She couldn't help thinking the rat leader was right. She hadn't done a very good job of looking after Marvin. She had guessed something was wrong that morning, but she hadn't done anything about it. If only she could make the rats listen. She noticed some of them eyeing her cat costume suspiciously.

'Listen!' she began, but Ruby interrupted her.

'If you want really want Marvin, you'll have come and get him!' the rat leader declared and, squishing the hamster into a ball, she gave him a swift push.

Marvin went rolling along the counter top like a furry football. Another rat stopped him before sending him spinning back again. The rats burst into peals of laughter as they sent the hamster whizzing back and forth.

'Stop! I'm getting dizzy,' squeaked Marvin.

Ruby chuckled and sent the little

hamster bouncing off the counter onto a table.

Kitty bounded across the café, reaching the counter in two enormous leaps. She pivoted around as Marvin rolled past. The hamster tumbled off the side of the table and went whizzing across the café floor.

Kitty leapfrogged over a table. Rats scurried everywhere, shrieking with excitement. Ruby marched through the middle of the crowd, yelling orders at them all.

'Marvin?' called Kitty. 'Where are you?'

Somersaulting over another table, she searched for Marvin among the mass of wriggling rats. She caught a flash of white fur and scooped the hamster from under a table. Marvin clung to her shoulder, shaking his head woozily.

'You shouldn't treat other creatures this way!' Kitty told the rats. 'You could have hurt him very badly.'

Ruby shrugged. 'He looks fine to

me. Anyway, we don't take orders from bossy old Cat Girls.'

Kitty was about to explain that she was just an ordinary girl with cat-like superpowers, but one of the rats gave a squeal and pointed at the window. Everyone swung round to see what he was looking at.

Figaro's black-and-white face was pressed

against the glass. The moonlight glinted on his whiskers. Pumpkin peered in beside him.

'More cats!' Ruby bounded on to the counter, grabbed a muffin and threw it at Kitty.

The other rats snatched cakes, brownies, and doughnuts from the counter and flung them wildly across the café. Kitty ducked, using her cat-like reflexes. Marvin squeaked and hid his face in her shoulder. A hail of cakes hit the window, leaving jam splodges and splatters of icing on the glass.

Kitty sheltered behind a table with Marvin. While she wasn't looking, Ruby jumped

down from the counter and grabbed
hold of the hamster. Then she rushed
to the door with the other rats
scampering after her.

'Wait!' called Kitty. 'Where are
you going?'

Ruby dragged Marvin outside, keeping a firm grip on his leg. Worried that the hamster might get hurt, Kitty waved to Figaro and Pumpkin to let the rats go. The creatures raced across the street, taking Marvin with them.

'Let me go!' squealed Marvin. 'I don't like adventures anymore.'

But the rats took no notice. Darting under the railings, they dashed down the grassy riverbank. Crowding around the water's edge, they chattered noisily and stamped their feet.

Kitty and her friends sneaked after them. The river gurgled and the moonlight drew a shimmering path across the water.

'What's going on, Kitty?' whispered Pumpkin.

'They're up to some new mischief no doubt,' grumbled Figaro.

'I'm not sure,' said Kitty. 'But I've got to get Marvin back!' She crept towards the cluster of rats, her eyes fixed on the fluffy white hamster in the middle.

Marvin looked around, his eyes wide.
Ruby still had a firm hold of his leg. 'Don't
worry, Marvy,' she said. 'Just keep
paddling and
you'll be fine.'

'Paddling!' squeaked Marvin. 'What do you mean?'

Kitty looked at the rats lined up by the water's edge and realized what was happening. 'Stop! He's a hamster and he can't swim.'

But it was too late.

'NOW!' yelled Ruby.

The rats leapt into the water with a huge splash. Marvin was knocked off the riverbank along with them. He bobbed under the surface for a moment and came up spluttering. 'Kitty!' he gasped. 'Please help me.'

'Hold on, Marvin!' Kitty raced down the bank, her eyes fixed on the little hamster.

She leaned out as far as she could, but Marvin was swept away by the river current. His eyes grew round with fright

and his tiny feet paddled frantically. He got stuck in a clump of water weed for a moment. Then the river pushed him on downstream.

The rats swam quickly across the river. When they got to the opposite bank, they jumped out and ran into the undergrowth.

'Come and find us when you want another adventure, Marvy!'

Ruby called back, carelessly.

Kitty ran along the riverbank, keeping up with Marvin as he was pushed forwards by the current. There had to be a way to reach the little hamster. She saw a footbridge and raced ahead to clamber over the railings.

Hooking her feet through the bars, Kitty swung over the water. She stretched out her arms as she sailed through the air. Marvin bobbed towards her, splashing

wildly. Kitty reached out and snatched him from the moonlit river. Then she somersaulted back on to the bridge and landed lightly on her feet.

Gently, she put Marvin down and crouched beside him. 'Are you all right?'

Marvin shivered. Water dripped off his fur and made a little puddle around his feet. 'I'm really cold!' he gasped. 'I wish I was back in my lovely warm cage.'

Kitty took a tissue out of her pocket and dried his coat. 'Why did you run away? I was so worried about you.'

Marvin sneezed. 'I liked my new home at first, but then I heard lots of strange noises. I started running on the wheel to block them out.'

'What sort of noises?' asked Kitty.

'There was a ticking and a whirring, and when it got dark they grew louder and louder!' explained Marvin. 'So I escaped from all the spooky sounds and when I got outside in the moonlight, I thought it would be lovely to have an adventure.'

'But why didn't you tell me about

the noises when I came to see you?'
asked Kitty.

'I don't know.' Marvin fidgeted
and looked at her shyly. 'I've never met
a human who can speak to animals
before.'

'Kitty!' Pumpkin came running on
to the bridge. 'We've just seen Pixie and
Katsumi and they said they'll help us
clear up the café.'

Kitty beamed. She could always
rely on her cat crew when she needed
a little extra help. 'I have a great idea!

Let's tidy up and then take Marvin
on a moonlit adventure.' She turned
back to the hamster. 'Would you like
that?'

'Oh, yes please!' Marvin said
eagerly. 'I'd like that more than
anything!'

Chapter

6

Kitty, Marvin, and the cats hurried back to the Cookies and Cream café. Katsumi, a sensible-looking tortoiseshell cat, had already begun sweeping crumbs from the floor. Pixie, a fluffy white cat with bright green eyes, skipped around the café mopping up splodges of icing. Pumpkin joined in by polishing the windows and Figaro inspected the tables to make sure each one was clean.

Kitty wrote a note to the café owner explaining what had happened and apologizing for the broken cakes. Then she turned to Marvin and smiled. 'Are you ready to have an adventure?'

'Yes, I am!' Marvin said, before adding, 'As long as there's no swimming in the river.'

'Don't worry. You won't have to do that!' Kitty settled Marvin on her shoulder. Then she closed the café door and led everyone to the backyard. Climbing onto some crates, they reached the roof and gazed out over the city.

The full moon hung over the rooftops. The river lay below them, glittering in the pale light. Boats bobbed up and down by the riverbank and the water reeds swayed gently in the breeze.

'Everything looks so pretty!' squeaked Marvin.

'It's a great night for an adventure and if you look really carefully you can see Emily's house all the way over there.' Kitty pointed to a little house

with a red roof
several streets away.
'It won't take us long to get
home.'

With her cat crew beside
her, Kitty skipped over
the rooftops.

She pointed out lots of interesting things to Marvin on the way—the park, the city museum, and the corner shop that sold her favourite strawberry sweets. Holding Marvin tightly, she somersaulted over a chimney pot and landed gracefully. The hamster yelled with delight.

They spotted Ruby and her rat gang outside the greengrocer's. The rats were pointing through the window at the vegetables and making disgusted faces.

'Hey, I've got an idea!' Kitty clambered down into the yard behind the shop. Picking up a box of mushy vegetables, she carried them back to the roof. 'These aren't fresh enough to be sold. Shall we show those rats what vegetables really taste like?'

'Yes, please!' Marvin giggled.

Kitty handed him a squashy tomato. Then she picked up an over-ripe pepper.

'Ready?' she asked, and the hamster nodded. Tiptoeing to the edge of the roof, Kitty made a long whistling sound.

The rats looked up.

'Hey, it's that Cat G-!' began one rat. Then a rotten pepper landed in his mouth.

Figaro, Pumpkin, and the others joined in, lobbing cucumbers,

mushrooms and carrots. The rats
licked the vegetable juice off their
whiskers and squealed in disgust.
They ran all over the place, bumping
into each other and falling over until
the pavement became a mass of
wriggling rats.

'What IS this!' said one, wiping
bits of carrot off his nose. 'It's
HORRIBLE!'

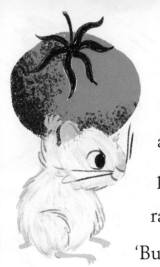

'I wouldn't usually approve of this kind of prank.' Figaro tossed some radishes at the fleeing rats. 'But one does have to make an exception for such naughty creatures.'

Ruby shook her fist at Kitty and her friends. 'Don't you dare throw that muck at me!' she began. 'I am Ruby the Magnificent—Eater of Cakes and Swallower of Sugar!'

With both arms, Marvin heaved

his squishy tomato high in the air. Then he threw it as hard as he could. The tomato landed with a squelch right on top of Ruby's head.

'YUCK!' screeched Ruby, waggling her head. Then she turned tail and ran off into the darkness.

Kitty giggled. 'Well, I think it's time to go home.'

They set off over the rooftops and reached Emily's house a few minutes later.

'Thanks for the adventure, Kitty!' Marvin said, with a yawn.

Kitty smiled. 'Shall we go inside and work out what those strange noises were? Then you can have a good night's sleep.'

'Can we help too?' Pumpkin asked eagerly.

'Of course you can!' Kitty opened the skylight and slipped inside. Pumpkin and Figaro followed, while Pixie and Katsumi decided to wait for them all on the roof.

Kitty took Marvin around the house, listening for ticking and creaking sounds. They found a ticking clock on the mantelpiece in the living room.

Then Pumpkin noticed that the refrigerator made a whirring sound and Figaro spotted a creaky step on the stairs.

'None of the sounds were scary after all!' said Marvin, as he snuggled down in his cozy cage. 'Oh dear, I've been so silly.'

'It must be tough getting used to living somewhere new, so don't be too hard on yourself,' said Kitty. 'Don't forget to call on me if you ever want another adventure.'

'Thank you, Kitty. I don't think I'll need another adventure for a long, long time!' Marvin took a piece of cucumber out of his bowl and snuggled down with his treat under the bedding.

Kitty closed the cage door and led her friends back through the skylight window. Pumpkin rubbed his eyes as

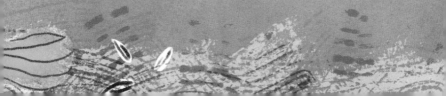

they climbed on to the roof to meet Pixie and Katsumi. 'I'm glad we saved Marvin, but I'm so sleepy now.'

'I'm absolutely exhausted!' Figaro yawned theatrically.

'I'm quite tired too,' meowed Pixie, and Katsumi agreed.

Kitty smiled. 'Why don't you all come home with me? You can curl up on my cushions and in the morning I'll cook you all mackerel for breakfast.'

Figaro perked up instantly. 'You have the most brilliant ideas, Kitty!'

'That's because she's the best Cat Girl in the world!' said Pumpkin.

Super Facts
About Cats

Super Speed

Have you ever seen a cat make a quick escape
from a dog? If so, you'll know that they can move
really fast—up to 30mph!

Super Hearing

Cats have an incredible sense of hearing
and can swivel their large ears to pinpoint
even the tiniest of sounds.

Super Reflexes

Have you ever heard the saying 'cats always
land on their feet'? People say this because
cats have amazing reflexes. If a cat is falling,
they can sense quickly how to move their
bodies into the right position to land safely.

Super Leaps

A cat can jump over eight feet high
in a single leap; this is due to its powerful
back leg muscles.

Super Vision

Cats have amazing night-time vision. Their
incredible ability to see in low light allows them
to hunt for prey when it's dark outside.

Super Smell

Cats have a very powerful sense of smell,
14 times stronger than a human's. Did you know
that the pattern of ridges on each cat's nose
is as unique as a human's fingerprint?

About the author

Paula Harrison

Before launching a successful writing career,
Paula was a Primary school teacher. Her years teaching
taught her what children like in stories and how
they respond to humour and suspense. She went on
to put her experience to good use, writing many
successful stories for young readers.

About the illustrator

Jenny Løvlie

Jenny is a Norwegian illustrator, designer,
creative, foodie, and bird enthusiast. She is fascinated
by the strong bond between humans and animals and
loves using bold colours and shapes in her work.

Love Kitty?
Why not try these too . . .

PILLGWENLLY